ONE

ARRIVAL

The only thing that can bring down the glory of a man is pride, not even your achievements can save you from damnation, if you're not saved. One needs to believe that in the chronicles of life, challenges are inevitable, if you're not prudent, you may fall and never rise again. Noah could only imagine the challenges that he will face this semester.

He gazed at the window, as objects flushed through his eyes and as the air rushed by the window.

"Chow-Chow! The train whistle echoed. Tim raised his lodges. He looked across the window once again, as he moved in linear formation with other passengers to step out of the train. A different set of people boarded the train, thereafter.

The entire train station was crowded, he couldn't hold sight of anyone, he held my lodges firmly due to the bad experience, he had the first time at the train station.

The train left the station. He looked around, and saw Peter, his friend, their course of study was civil engineering, it's tedious and requires one to apply a grease of rigidity to study and this was their third year at Albert Vincent University. Although, they never lived in the same lodge outside the University. Peter was a stammerer. He was five feet away from where Noah stood.

"Hey, Peter!" Noah waved his right hand to get his attention.

"Hello, Noah! It's nice to see you again. How have you been?" Peter asked. As they embraced each other.

Peter smelt like coffee, he was not impressed from the look on his face. It seems something else must have made him feel this way.

"It's all good at the other side, you know, family, the care and love, they show, seeing me again, after a while."

"How about you? How did you spend your summer? Noah asked.

"Am just trying, to get back to my feet. Since the demise of my father, life has not been beautiful. Am only coping with the situation of things." Peter said.

"It's well, my friend." Noah replied.

Noah had no words of comfort, the least he could do at that moment was to tap him on the shoulder as a sign of hope.

"Who are you waiting for?" Noah asked.

"No one really, am just been thoughtful on how I will manage the little money, I have at hand to board a taxi and have something to eat later." He said soberly.

He noticed, how Noah lifted his right hand to his left breast pocket, to bring out a sum of money. He interrupted. "Ahh! Noah, don't bother about that."

"Am your friend, more importantly, we need to look after each other, you know." Noah smiled at him.

"Thank you so much."Peter said softly. As he gazed at the money.

As they walked out of the train station, they talked and laughed about other things. The look on their faces will tell anyone, they were glad to see each other.

Noah stretched out his hand to board a taxi, he noticed that someone was staring at me from a distance, ignorance was the only option, he had.

Noah noticed that Peter starring at the pair of shoe, he wore, because they appeared to be expensive.

They entered the taxi. Noah told the taxi driver to take them to Central Avenue, where most of the students lived outside the University.

As they approached Central Avenue, there was a road block up ahead before the entrance. Noah wondered what could have prompted this action.

"Please Sir, I cannot go any further." The driver said. Peter startled at him.

"Ok, let's step out of the car." Noah said.

Noah paid the taxi fare and the taxi driver, drove off. They stood by the road side and watched the taxi drive out of the area.

"Why will you be in a haste to step out of the car? Don't you know, you deserve some explanation from that Mickey Mouse?" Peter arrogantly said.

Astonished at what he said, Noah turned towards him in a state of surprise.

"You don't have to be rude. As far as I can tell there's a reason behind the road block." Noah replied.

As they approached the road block, there were security guards, present, as they were dressed in their uniform.

One of the security guards enquired for their identification card and their purpose of coming to the avenue. They deliberately identified with him and called their landlord's for further clarification, in order to pass through the road block.

After they successfully cleared from the road block. They moved together to an extent and parted ways.

But, Noah was bothered about the sudden closure. If not for the fact that Central Avenue had previous records of criminal cases.

TWO

PREPARATION

The birds chirped, the cock crowed, footsteps of people within as their flapped alongside, the sound of a car engine, steaming up.

Peter woke up late. He felt sorry for himself because, this was not the normal time, he wakes up daily.

"A new day for a new challenge," he soloquised.

He observed his quiet time, dressed his bed, took his bucket and other toiletry.

"Good Morning Sir."

"Good Morning Noah, how are you?" His landlord asked.

"Am fine Sir."

"Are you not late for your lectures , this morning?".

"No Sir, I only have a test today by 1pm." The landlord nodded in acceptance.

"Ok, goodluck." The landord replied.

Noah lived in a native compund, were people of diverse backgrounds lived with their families. The only quick means a tenant can take a bath was in the early hours of the morning by 5am, **"the faster you wake, the better for you"** was the motto.

His neighbours are busy people, most of them are traders, bankers and teachers. They lived in this kind of places due to the high cost of living in town. In order to meet up with their needs and family demands.

After a warm bath, Noah had breakfast, dressed up and moved out of his lodge.

Four blocks away from his lodge. He sighted a group of people chattering under a Mango tree, they looked rugged in appearance, they paid no attention to side walks, as they were conversing.

Peter was in their midst. "What is he doing over there?" Noah thought.

Noah bowed down his head like he was thinking of how the stones on the ground were made?" Unfortunately, Peter sighted him.

"Noah, are you going to school?" Peter asked from a distance.

"Yes, I am heading for class, I thought you knew we had test on Calculus today, that is Engr. Felix's course, by 1pm at CES Hall?" Scratching his head in confusion, he couldn't respond quickly.

"Ehmm... Yes, I guess, I heard about it. I will meet you in class."

"Ok, see you there."

"Hey, Noah, I want to let you know that these guys are good, they really want to help me out financially, am glad to be among them, truly."

"I can only advice you to be careful and be positive."

"You don't need to worry. It's alright." Peter said. As he bounced back to the Mango tree.

Most of the time, when a group of people gather this way, there's something fishy, but not withstanding let it be for the greater good or something bad.

THREE

REVELATION TO CALL UP

Two months to the semester exam. Series of test have been taken in some courses, assignments and practical's too. The semester is too jammed with a lot of activities, including campus fellowship activities and academic activities.

It was Friday. Students do take Friday as part of the weekend. From Noah's schedule, he had no activity for the weekend.

At the end of the day, he returned back to my lodge, did the regular tidying, prepared stew, which he would utilize during the weekend.

He had a terrible dream concerning Peter, that Friday night.

In a class room setting, he saw Peter knelling down in front of the class room, as everyone mocked him, threw dirt on him, spat on him and others were beating him up.

Right there. was a man who stood at the entrance door of the class. He had an ugly appearance. He pointed his finger towards Peter and laughed ceaselessly as Peter was being humiliated. Noah couldn't understand what was happening. As he raised his voice to call out his name, the reception was not clear enough, he struggled several times to call out his name, all to no avail.

Someone tapped him from behind; it was a man on white apparel.

He woke with heat gliding through his whole body. He prayed about it, it seemed the strength to pray was not forthcoming.

Hence, he decided to visit Peter the next day.

Peter lived in a comfortable lodge. He was surprised to see Noah this early before mid-day at his lodge. He welcomed him into his room.

Peter sat on an ancient fancy couch, with a cold bottle of soft drink on the bench at his left hand side and a glass on his right hand, he drank like he drank to the taste of victory.

"Yes, how's your weekend? Am surprised you came to my place this early, is everything alright?" Peter asked.

"All is well, no friction of problems of any kind. "

"You're not looking bad. Good student, is not that am a bad one, is just that I need to hustle and get some money, for me to go to school, as you know it and fix myself properly."

"Really? That's good for you, what about those guys?" Noah asked.

"Ok, those guys? Hmmm... their hustling motivation inspires me to be better than I am, if you understand." Peter smiled.

"I had a bad dream last night about you, I dare you to listen to what I have to say."

"Go ahead." Peter said.

"In my dream last night, I was walking into the class room, I saw you knelling in front of the class room, our course mates mocked you, threw dirt's, spat, slapped You, behold a man was standing at the entrance door of the class room, he looks ugly, dark skin, he pointed his finger at you and laughed at You ceaselessly, as you were being disgraced by the entire class. As I tried calling out your name, I couldn't hear myself, someone tapped me from behind. Immediately, I returned back to reality."

"Thank you. All this long story." Peter sighed and waved his head with a smile on his face as he leaned back and laughed.

"Noah! Noah!! Noah!! How many times did I call out your name? I don't believe in junk talks like this. Please, take it back." He paused. "I thought you had something better to offer. Am your friend, but, you don't dream for me, I do have dreams. So... don't tell me such gibberish again."

"You have to listen to me... These words I speak to you are not fabricated. I speak the truth to you. You need to be extremely careful, I don't know what you're planning to do or who you're involved with for a business or anything else, you need to be careful."

"Are you not taking this seriously?" Noah asked.

"This sounds absolutely stupid to me or whatever it is you've said." Peter said.

"It's not stupid," Noah argued. "But it's alright. If you don't adhere."

Noah felt he had made a ridiculous dopy fool of himself. He rose up to go.

"One more detail. Try to make it to church service on Sunday."Noah said.

"Alright! Alright!!" Peter said. As he rose up and slammed the door.

FOUR

PROPHECY

As the sun shone brightly above the skies on a Sunday Morning.

In an auditorium filled with worshippers, harmony, fresh air, happy faces, colorful dresses, voices in excitement as the instrumentals played to the tone of the melody rendered by the praise team. It starred the atmosphere in the congregation as people lifted up their voices and sang to the Glory of God. This was the Glory of God Church; it's situated some blocks away from my lodge in Central Avenue.

"Noah, you're already here." Peter said. As he stretched out his hand for a hand shake.

"Yes brother, welcome to the House of God," Noah replied.

All of a sudden there was absolute tranquility as the minister reached the pulpit.

"Thank You, the praise team for the beautiful melodies, you've rendered and to the congregation you've all praised and danced to the Glory of God." Pastor John looked around for a while.

"Now the Lord is that Spirit: and where the Spirit of the Lord is, there is liberty," "said Paul wrote to the people at Corinth. 2 Corinthians 3:17." Noah nodded.

"Please, bow your heads, as we pray briefly for the word of God, we're about to hear from our Creator, Master, Guardian and Saviour, that he alone will lead us to the light of the truth in his word!" said Pastor John.

Meanwhile, before the prayers were concluded. Noah noticed that Peter was dozing already. He quickly tapped him on the shoulder, to bring him back to order.

"Amen! Amen!! Yes Lord! Yes Lord! Peter exclaimed. As he raised up his head, he immediately noticed that the congregation was silent, as they were still in the mood of prayer. He quietly bowed down his head in shame.

"We pray in Jesus Name. Amen!"

"Praise the Lord! Hallelujah!"

"Hallelujah!! Amen. The congregation responded interactively, as they lifted up their heads in anticipation to hear God's word.

"The word of the Lord is a two edged sword, listen, respect God's word and you will receive what GOD has to say concerning you this moment." said Pastor John.

As the man of God continued, Inaudibly, Peter whispered to Noah.

"Noah, I like that girl."

"Shhh... Focus and Listen to the man of God," Noah said. Peter sighed.

Fifteen Minutes later, the sermon continued. As there was absolute tranquility as the man of God ministered.

"The Lord ministered to me, someone in the congregation is about to be disgraced, be careful, be careful. Be what? Careful, listen. Don't joke with the revelation concerning you, pray that you may not be used by the devil, for he is only concerned to steal, kill and to destroy, John 10:10. The minister also added, "How that by revelation he made known unto me the mystery, Ephesians 3:3. Therefore be careful."

"Did you hear? What the man of GOD just said?"

"Nah!" Peter reacted blindly.

After a while, Pastor John, dismissed the church service.

"May the Peace of the Lord be with you all." The congregation responded, "Amen!".

The Church service was over, as everyone dispatched to their various destinations.

Noah stepped out of the Church hall with Peter. Before them was Freda, the assistant choir mistress, for the youth wing. She was good looking and beautiful.

"Good day Sister in Christ," Peter softly said.

"Remain blessed brother," Freda replied.

"Peter! Peter!! Let's get going. Noah shouted.

"Chill bro, let me finish." As he winked me and displayed a gesture for Noah to calm down.

"Thanks for the contact, I hope to see you again." Peter Said.

"As far as you promise to attend choir practice regularly, you can buzz me, anytime." Freda said, as she gave a dashing smile to Peter.

"Alright dear, I will definitely." As he moved towards Noah.

"You don't seem to understand the importance of a woman in a man's life, you are just pretending. You have eyes man, you need to get hold of these sweet strawberries. Don't say, I did not tell you." He quaked Noah.

Noah pouted at him, as he seemed to have become a counselor on relationship matters.

"I understand what you mean. Currently, that's the least of my worries."

"You can say whatever you like." Peter said.

He reached out for his phone in his pocket and dialed a number. He was actually trying to call his newly found church girl, as starred at the piece of paper he used to copy the phone number.

"Yes, tis I Peter, this is my phone number, please save it."

"Ok, I will, bye..." Freda said. The call ended. Noah chuckled because he knew this one will be difficult for Peter.

"Have you been preparing for the exam?" Noah asked.

"Ehmm... No, not really, it's just that sometimes... It's difficult for me to study. Honestly, I've not bought some of the recommended textbooks for the semester." Peter said.

"It's ok. Remember, that it's never too late to study and get your materials, the earlier the better." Noah advised. Peter nodded.

"Yes, I understand. See you tomorrow in class." Peter said. As he opened the gate to enter into his lodge.

FIVE

ESCAPE FOR LIFE

Two weeks later, the school management releeased a tenetative examination time table. In order to gear up students to read ahead for their forth coming examination.

More so, the school mangement declared one week of free lecture, as it was declared on Friday.

Noah returned to his lodge at exactly 3pm. He was exhausted and laid on my bed.

"I need to rest for the moment. Besides, the human body is not a fire wood. I also need to do justice to study for my forth coming examination. For there's reward for hardwork." He soloquished. As he starred at the ceiling of his room.

Seventy-five minutes later, he woke up and quickly checked the time on his wall clock, it was 4;25pm.

"Ahh! My head aches." Noah exclaimed. He stretched his hand from the bed to grab his phone on the table. He dialed Peter's number, as he wanted him to come along with him to attend the youth fellowship. Unfortunately, Peter's number was unreachable.

"Perhaps, it's a network issue." Noah concluded.

He quickly rushed to take a quick bath, grabbed his materials and left..

The fellowship came to a conclusion late in the evening hours. James, the youth leader, urged Noah to wait for him, so they can go together.

As they walked eight blocks away from from the church. Suddenly, three men with flashlights drew nearer to them, as they were close enough.

"Stop there! If you take one more step, I will shot you. Get on your knees now." One of them said rudely.

The one in the middle was a mesomorph, taller than the other two, he had a gun and he seems to be the boss.

" Boss, what do we do with them?

"Pigeon, collect their phones.

"Sparrow, take off their belts and shoes. The boss commanded. They obeyed as if they were accustomed to receiving orders and obeyed them.

"Give me the offering."

"Ahh! Please Sir, it's the Lord's" James said.

"Shut your mouth! I am your lord now, be quick and hand hand it over." As the boss pointed the gun towards Noah.

"I will Sir, take it all." James said. His hands were shaking tremendously as he stretched them out.

"Good for you. Sparrow! Move this other idiot aside, let's deal with this stubborn one."

"Be quiet and move." As he dragged Noah 3 feet away from James. "Kneel down and close your eyes." Sparrow said.

Noah slightly opened his eyes. He saw that they were only focused on James. He rose up gradually and tip-toed backwards. He gapped the, a bit, about twelve feet and ran away to call for help.

Pigeon pointed his flashlight at the supposed position where Noah stood, but couldn't see him there.

"Boss ooo... That boy is not there."

"Where is he?"

"I don't know, ask Sparrow." Pigeon said.

"Sparrow! Where is your prisoner?"

"Boss, he was right there, I threatened him not to make a move, maybe... he... disappeared." Sparrow said.

"You're a fool! Find him." The boss said angrily.

Meanwhile, Noah ran as fast as he can to Central Avenue Police Station to call for help. He was gripped with fear, drenched by heat, he stammered vigorously in fear, as he tried to explain the situation to the Police officers.

Before the Police officers could arrive at the scene, James was lying on the ground half dead.

SIX

ECHOING SHOCK

Three weeks later, the semester exam was over. Noah had no idea, what was coming for him, as he was gearing up to travel back home, next week, Monday.

Meanwhile, Peter was nowhere to be found even in campus, at his lodge and his phone number was not even reachable.

It rained heavily on Monday morning. Noah had woken up early, as at 4:30am to prepare. He wanted to board the first train in the morning. The morning train was to leave the station by 6:30am. Although, he had already bought his ticket during the weekend.

He packed his luggage, cleaned his room, prepared himself and was only waiting for the rain to stop.

5:45am, the rain ceased. He raised his luggage to step out. Suddenly, he heard a blast sound outside, it sounded like the gate in the compound, was struck down by a fierce wind.

"Catch him! Chase him!! Beat him up!!! Burn him!!!! Don't let him out of your sight. He thinks he's smart, you will not live to tell the story." Someone voiced out.

The voice emanated within the compound premises; Noah dropped his luggage and stepped out. Behold, a large crowd, some with clubs, big stones, machetes, they formed a contorted circle. The crowd enclosed more and more to the centre, while others struggled to reach their weapons to the person at the centre of the circle.

Noah watched from a distance, while others quaked Noah as they moved towards the scene with their weapons.

"Every day for the thief, one day for the owner of the house." Someone from the crowd quoted.

The crowd showed no mercy, they mounted on him without compassion.

Noah retained his distance from the crowd.

"Noah! Four able bodied men came into the compound as early as 3:00am, they came to kidnap the landlord ooo! The rain disappointed them; they did not succeed at the end. It's only this one that was not lucky enough to run away. If not that, Amos, the security man, raised an alarm, when he saw them as they climbed the fence to escape, no one could have known," Andrew, the Landlord's son narrated.

"He will receive his due reward, you people should plunge him. No mercy." Noah said. He moved closer to the scene, lo and behold, it was Peter, battered, drenched in blood. He was lying down on the ground like a lifeless chicken.

For a moment, Noah was dumb and couldn't get hold of himself. His eyes became cloudy; he was shocked and was shivering. He left the scene in agony.

This is how you ended up, after biding you to adhere to the revelations... and advi...ce..." Noah soberly shredded.

Tears rolled down my cheeks, seeing Peter's lifeless body in the wet mud.